For Syd Walker –
a belated thank you

Copyright © 1997 by Ken Brown
The rights of Ken Brown to be identified as the author and illustrator of this work have
been asserted by him in accordance with the Copyright, Designs and Patents Act, 1988.
First published in Great Britain in 1997 by Andersen Press Ltd., 20 Vauxhall Bridge Road,
London SW1V 2SA. Published in Australia by Random House Australia Pty., 20 Alfred
Street, Milsons Point, Sydney, NSW 2061. All rights reserved. Colour separated in
Switzerland by Photolitho AG, Zürich. Printed and bound in Italy by Grafiche AZ, Verona.

10   9   8   7   6   5   4   3   2   1

British Library Cataloguing in Publication Data available.
ISBN 0 86264 751 7

This book has been printed on acid-free paper

Mucky Pup

Written and illustrated by
Ken Brown

𝔸

Andersen Press · London

Mucky pup was having a wonderful time. He emptied the
wastepaper basket, he cleaned out the coal skuttle,

he rearranged the tablecloth and shook the cushions - what fun.

The farmer's wife didn't
think it was such fun.
"Oh you mucky pup,"
she cried. "Out you go."

But mucky pup wanted to play.
He saw the cockerel.
"Will you play with me?" he asked.
"Cockadoodledon't be stupid," crowed the cockerel.
"I'm a beautiful cockerel - you're just a mucky pup."

Pup saw the duckling.
"Will you play with me?" he asked.
"You must be quack, quack, quackers," quacked the duckling.
"I'm a fluffy duckling - you're just a mucky pup."

Pup saw the cat.
"Will you play with me?" he asked.
"How perrrfectly ridiculous," purred the cat.
"I'm a handsome cat - you're just a mucky pup."

Pup saw the horse.
"Will you play with me please, please?"
"Nay, nay," neighed the horse.
"I'm a magnificent shire-horse - you're just a mucky pup."

Pup was sad. Who would play with him?
Perhaps they were right after all - he was too mucky.
He wandered outside into the yard.

Suddenly a snout appeared through the bars of the gate.
"Hello," said the piglet. "Will you play with me?"
"No," said Pup. "I'm just a mucky pup."
"But I'm just a mucky pig," said the piglet. "Let's play in the mucky mud!"

And that's just what they did.

Until...

SPLASH!

"Pup, mucky pup!" called the farmer's wife. "Bathtime!"
But mucky pup didn't need a bath.

He was a good, clean, clever pup,
and he settled down by the fire
to dream about playing
with his mucky piglet
friend tomorrow.